THE FOREST
OF DEAD
CHILDREN

The Forest of Dead Children

by

Andrew Hook

BLACK SHUCK
SHADOWS

Black Shuck Books
www.BlackShuckBooks.co.uk

First published in the UK by Black Shuck Books, 2019

978-1-913038-14-4

This book is dedicated to my children,
Sarah & Cora, without whom

Shipwrecked
in the Heart
of the City

Interviewer: Suppose your house were on fire and you
could remove only one thing.
What would you take?
Jean Cocteau: I would take the fire

The baby was dead inside her.

Standing in the shower, water jets gave
punctuation to her distended stomach. Her left
hand rested just below her breasts, atop the
bump; her right hand above her pubis,
cradling.

Her face was wet. She remembered her
cousin's child, age two, placing potatoes down
the front of its baby-gro, emulating its mother's
second pregnancy. It was as though the pox had
her. Their laughter had been pure, squealing
tyres. The child thoughtfully added more

potatoes. An explosion in a fat suit. It was then that Emily wanted her own pregnancy.

The porthole window forced a corridor of sunlight, penetrating the steam like a laser beam. Ephemeral rays danced with the watery wisps: a kaleidoscope in sight. The angle shaved the top of her head. She raised her eyes, watched it pass over her like Mike Teevee in *Charlie and the Chocolate Factory*. Where it touched the back wall the light and condensation resembled a circular patch of bubblewrap, or maybe a child's embossed sticking plaster.

These moments adopted meaning external to the physicality of their presence. Sharply she switched the lever from on to off. A thousand snakes ceased hissing. Cool air immediately raised goosebumps on her skin. She stood a moment longer, her hands returned to their position. She almost didn't dare breathe the word *kick*, as if to allow the thought that there might be no response would in itself change a status from alive to dead. She held it back, but it was there and had been there for eighteen hours. Without towelling herself dry she returned to her bedroom.

Topography: a shock of dyed-blonde hair,

soiled at the roots; the valley bordered by her clavicle; her breasts with their mountaintops; the convex once concave; the stubble of her bush; those stilts; her toes, painted, pointing upwards like tiny grave markers. She lay backwards on the cool silk bedding. Examined the ceiling. Remembered.

Another one inside her. His face caught between pleasure and pain. Such a dichotomy of expression.

She wondered what had become of him.

Death wasn't simply an absence of life. It was an almost. The unhaled breath.

Her right hand began to move rhythmically over her mound. *C'mon sleeper. Wake up.*

~

The city is a complex entity. Layered personal histories, jumbled objects in a toy box. Lives were haphazard, tightrope existences. He moved through it like a wader. People sloughed aside him. Lights blinked repeatedly as though responses to abstract thought. He considered life might either be an interlinked preordained process or simply chaos. If he were to say he preferred chaos then he knew he would be lying.

Everyone needed something to be tied to.

In his room, silent, with his hand held to his stomach, the umbilical cord a fat intestine-like rope in his grip, he wondered where it might lead.

In one corner, his shoes sat on a wooden chair, his shirt and jacket thrown over the back. His underwear revealed the invisible man on the carpet. To one side, an empty wardrobe yawned one half of its double doors. A mirror over a dressing table was tarnished around the metal screws that fixed it four-cornered to the wall. He listened quietly for the squeaks that might reveal these objects as sentient. But within his room the only obstruction to perfect silence was muffled underwater thunder.

Whenever he tried to think about it...

...and then he would return.

He stood. Ran a hand through his hair. The mirror reflected a chunk of stomach, a jigsaw piece that tailed away. The cord hung down to the base of his penis, which, in an inevitable comparison, itself extended further downwards as though they were components in a knot of sausages. He pulled on his clothes, roughly. Tension ran around the outside of his skin as though the crux of it were inside. He shuddered.

He didn't want it to end. Not yet. Not when he had barely begun to understand it.

No one locked their doors. He left the apartment, took the stairs. Was reminded of a photograph he believed he had once seen of a cat ascending when it might also have been descending. Outside the sky was darkened: colourbox absent. He walked a couple of blocks with his head down. Entered one of the bars and ordered milk. Sucking it through the straw reassured him: a native who knew the way.

He wiped the front of his mouth with the back of his hand. Saw a line of red amid the white, like the telltale graze of lipstick on a collar: the intimation of threat.

~

Emily said nothing at the office. She fielded questions over gestation in her normal manner: with a smile and a sense of weariness. There was no question that the baby was dead. There had been no bleeding, no cramps. It didn't matter. She hadn't made the third trimester. She would keep on going until her next hospital appointment. Nothing could be done. She broke with the thought of not maintaining the illusion.

She understood the definition of a *dead weight*.

"Not getting enough sleep?"

"Hmmm?"

She raised her head from her desk with some embarrassment. A yellow Post-It note stuck to her cheek. When she pulled it away strands of hair popped firecracker noises.

"I know it's your break, but you might find it easier to rest in the chill-out room."

A wan smile passed between herself and her manager, as though it were on loan to both.

Emily stood, rested a hand on her desk, the other reflexing stomach-wards. She drew it back, slo-mo, petrified to touch. If her manager noticed the movement he paid no heed to it. Her feet carried her to the partitioned space where her co-workers at lunch – reading books, thumb-flicking phone screens – pushed food into open mouths. Charlie was at the vending machine, rocking it back and forth, one palm at the top right-hand corner, the other obscuring the panel reading *Do not rock this machine*. It listed a number for the maintenance team who no one ever saw.

He abandoned the effort. "Nothing ever

comes out," he said. He threw a glance around the room which no one caught.

Emily sank into a reconditioned sofa, attracting the well-meaning looks of those favourable to babies yet aggrieved by maternity leave. She found herself pulling a phone from her pocket, scrolling through the lives of others. Traction. Attraction. Words scrambled in her head. She closed her eyes. Concentrated on tiny pinpricks of light, discarded galaxies. She imagined being carried away by the backs of her eyelids, somersaulting her inside her body, cartwheeling an existential journey until she saw the nub of the problem: suspended in aspic, her baby. Roughly hewn, partly sewn. When she opened her eyes, tears fell out.

You alright love?

Hormones.

You look a bit peaky.

She heard sentences but these were disparate from those present. It was as though she were in a waiting room. Establishing camaraderie through temporary circumstances which wouldn't be replicated out of that scenario.

She felt isolated.

She was alone.

~

He watched the dancers ambivalently. They worked the poles like puppets whose strings were released then repeatedly caught. Knee-bending actions. Tiny briefs cut skin like wires through putty. Should these dancers harden their scars would be well-worn. Should he harden he would be surprised.

Occasionally he spat into an ashtray. Dark blood caught dog-ends, briefly fixed them with life's semblance. He considered fire, then; how it contained movement without thought. He returned to the dancers.

Outside there was always outside. Something should be in the sky. He pushed his hands into his jacket pockets. In another life there would be a wallet, keys, coins. In another life.

He began to trap the thought by trying not to think of it, but the very act of not thinking gave credence to its existence. And – via that spiral – he soon forgot what he had been trying to forget.

He walked by the docks. Water soothed him somewhat. He imagined inflating a balloon and then climbing inside, pushing his hands against the skein.

Someone was talking about memory. *I can only remember when I sing.*

Someone replied: *that's just annoying. Can't you sing in your head?*

Have you ever heard me sing in my head?

From time to time he felt tugged to join those utterances. It was rare for more than two people to converse simultaneously. Once he saw a small group of them: five, possibly six. All talking together, their umbilical cords on clear display. Within the group, two looked like the other, as did another two. There was something alien – unlikely – about the ensemble. One of them appeared sick.

He blew into his hands. Moved on.

At some point he found he had returned to his apartment. Slowly he removed his clothing, placed it on the chair, on the floor. For a short while he stood inside the empty wardrobe. Metal coathangers were moulded around a wooden pole. He thought of the dancers, sideways. He reached out his hands and pressed them against the surface of the wood. If he pushed a little harder he too might find a memory to sing.

On the bed he touched his cord. He considered it an indicator of his health. In the pale light it seemed disfigured. It *was* the light, he decided, preferring to ignore madness. As usual when he closed his eyes he didn't sleep.

Muffled thunder rushed his ears, a storm in a subway.

At some point, he knew, something would have to give.

Everything known would be swept away.

He touched key parts of his body and found no response.

~

Emily stood belly-proud in front of the mirror. She could hear her cousin's children playing downstairs. It wasn't clear how she felt about that. An ear rested on her stomach. On her hands and knees her cousin listened.

"What are you expecting to hear?"

Her cousin looked up. "I don't know. Gurgling?" The way she said it should have carried a smile but didn't. Then she said: "You know, intestinal gurgling."

"It's been eight days," Emily said.

"If you were worried you should have called me before. If you were *that* worried you would have called a doctor. Call it intuition, but it says a lot that you didn't."

But Emily knew why she hadn't. She couldn't face the unbridled hostility of devastating shock.

"Maybe it sleeps during the day and wakes at night when you're asleep."

"You know that can't be true."

"Jemima didn't move for this long once."

Emily shrugged the placebo.

Her cousin made a moue. "See a doctor then."

"My ultrasound is Wednesday."

"Then Wednesday it is!"

Downstairs the interaction between the two children was raised a notch as they systematically attempted to destroy one another.

Emily waved as their car pulled out of the drive. She had worked hard to get where she was. All her neighbours were – or had been – married. She was the singleton on the block. Initially she hadn't cared for the glances towards her pregnant state. Now she sought them. But the street was deserted. Televisions simulated movement behind net curtains. She didn't want sympathy. She wanted pregnancy.

The wind caught the door as she closed it, the

skin on her fingertips losing a few cells to the outside just as she was inside.

Wednesday would come too soon.

She walked through to the kitchen, took out a cereal bowl and placed it on the table. Positioned a bottle of milk to one side, and a rectangular packet on the other with its stylised yellow, green and red cockerel given life by the brain's desire to find meaning where there was no sense. Or sense where there was no meaning.

She watched those objects for the remainder of the afternoon, until her back cramped and her legs flickered and she lost all reality of herself.

~

In the park a giant chessboard was marked out in white and pale-pink paving stones. He played against himself, hefting the pieces which were almost his size from one square to another. Perspective distorted. Only from a height could the game make sense. So he took it one move at a time, occasionally confusing white with black, until only two pieces remained on the board.

A white queen and a black pawn.

The sides of the white queen were greased in the blood from his hands.

He couldn't have taken two kings, he knew that.

Benches lined the park. Grass was verdant. A small crowd had gathered, joined by his play. Umbilical cords swung in circles, decapitated umbrellas. He noticed a couple physically joined at the hip, yet only one had a cord. The man on the left was dessicated, a withered being, pale and lifeless. But he was held steady by the other man who didn't mind sharing the burden.

He knocked over the queen and raised the pawn.

Nothing happened.

And when it didn't, he walked to the nearest establishment and sank a glass of milk.

The glass returned to the counter with an imprint of blood.

He had to talk to someone. Back in the park, the sky had darkened further. There was a rumbling: a bowling ball down an alley. Everyone had gone. He found himself running, from block to block, tripping over paving stones, falling, picking himself up before he hit the ground. His eyes scanned for street signs but there were none. Never had been.

The door to his apartment was ajar. He

couldn't remember locking it. This was another memory he needed to sing. He pushed open the door, found no one. He had expected someone. Someone should have been waiting.

There was nothing for it. He took off his clothes, pulled the sheets from the bed until all that remained was the bare wooden frame. He curled up, foetus-like, his head bent in supplication, his knees close to his chest, his arms tight, little fists tensed as if expecting to box. After a moment he felt for his umbilical cord where it was squashed between one leg and his stomach, and he straightened it, pointed it away from his body, as though it were an arrow to another place.

He remained this way.

Waiting for something to happen.

Until even his corporeality wasn't in his memory.

~

If it were a television show then Emily didn't care for the picture: grainy, indistinct, fixed.

Her belly was slippery. She could smell rubber.

She had obliterated every emotion apart from the one she had managed to keep hidden:

hope. Under the gaze of the ultrasound she allowed it to flutter.

Later, in a room with two chairs. An arm bidding her to sit.

Outside, weather pushed at the glass, threatened to enter.

Sounds reverberated: the wheel of a trolley, the indistinct chatter of the nurses, someone peeing into a cylinder, the scratch of pen on paper, jostling.

His face was round. An accent matched his goatee. He sat opposite.

This is what he said:

I'm sorry Emily. The pregnancy terminated in the womb.

But she didn't hear this.

Instead she heard:

Emily. Emily? Here, here was your son.

The Rhythm of Beauty

Before his perspective shifted, Frisch recalled cycling home one evening, the waning sun transforming the pink cycle route into an arterial track against the surrounding black asphalt. He found himself ambivalent about his day, which had neither attribute of interesting or dull, whilst the repetition of movement was anathema to memory, each turn of a bicycle wheel erasing his journey in the moment of creating it.

As usual near the traffic lights he joined a queue of other cyclists, most wearing tight reflective clothing; helmeted and cammed. Frisch preferred the freedom of the casual rider, having decided some time ago that to protect himself against injury did, in fact, invite it, that padding and plastic tempted fate and afforded petrol-driven drivers a reassurance that should they nudge an elbow with a wing-mirror then the cyclist in question would be *ok*, cocooned as they might be within a protective skin. Whereas Frisch, with his regular clothing and earphones his only headgear, was given a wider berth and therefore a safer passage. Besides, Frisch reasoned, should he be knocked from his bike he would rather exit this life to a soundtrack of his choosing. There was a pleasure to be had in imagining a concerned pedestrian removing one of the earphones to hear a tinny rendition increasing in sound and definition as curiosity overcame them to hear what Frisch had been listening to at the moment of his death.

On this evening – four riders ahead – a woman pressed against her pedals at the change to a green light, her rear lifting slightly for leverage as she made the effort, her speed tempered by the child in the baby seat behind her, its head lolling from side to side within a loosely fitting helmet. As each successive cyclist caught and passed her, Frisch noted each afford a smile at the sleeping child, whose neck appeared to be constructed of elastic as it bobbed the head back and forth in a deelybopper movement. Frisch considered each of these smiles together with the almost muscle-less state of the child's body, superimposing a terror that the child might actually be dead, that what the cyclists considered to be the rhythm of beauty was actually occasioned by the woman refusing to succumb to the truth of her child's passing, contending to perform her daily routine as if the child were still alive. Frisch imagined speeding up and cycling beyond the twosome, gathering courage to look the child direct in the eye only to find the whites rolled back into a lifeless grey visage.

With this idea taking hold, Frisch held back, his legs seeming to make inexorably slow movements to stay behind the grotesquery, pinning him between truth and fiction in a self-perpetuating circle, much as his wheel movement simultaneously drove him forwards just as the tarmac shifted back.

It was during this *danse macabre* of Frisch's imagination that he woke.

~

The sound might have been distilled from the very fear of his dream. In the adjacent room his daughter eviscerated a scream. Frisch's heart loop-de-looped and his wife dug him in the ribs.

"She's at it again," Madeleine said, bunching herself up and rubbing her eyes.

"Should I go to her?"

"What's the point? Let's wait it out."

They fell silent within their room, whilst the tumult continued on the other side of the wall, Esme battling what appeared to be a physical demon, incoherent drama forcing itself from her mouth, snatches of words amidst a gale of noise. Frisch felt guilty; waiting for the act to subside was a paradigm of boredom. It was impossible to return to sleep until Esme settled down, yet staying awake at the point of exhaustion held its own demands. Eventually the familiar sound of her leaving her bed, coupled with stampeding footsteps signifying the destination of their room, brought her into his arms with all the reluctance of a boxer being held when wanting to return to the ring.

Against Madeleine's wishes, Frisch attempted comfort, Esme hitting out and screaming at those attempts, until eventually he stood and swore, throwing her down onto the duvet in exasperation, at which moment she closed her eyes and immediately fell asleep.

When Esme had first experienced her night terrors, Frisch and Madeleine had been equally afraid. With wide open eyes Esme appeared to be awake, yet her reactions to their cosseting suggested she had no idea who they were, their ineffectual attempts to soothe her only exacerbating the situation. In deep-sleep haze, Frisch entertained the possibility of Esme being possessed, his suggestions rebuked angrily by Madeleine as fanciful nonsense, even as he equated his wife's vehemence as a denial of the truth. In wakeful hours, Frisch's perception was far more reasoned. He was aware of the concept of night terrors, and whilst they were uniquely disturbing, the knowledge that Esme had no memory of them went some way to alleviate his concerns.

Nevertheless, there were some degrees difference between understanding and acceptance, and whilst Esme's return to sleep might be swift and trouble-free, the same could not be said of Frisch, whose heart hammered at the stress of sudden awakening and whose imagination took much longer to subside into the slip of dream.

Esme was six years old. When Frisch quizzed her the following morning about nightmares, her reaction was the same as always:

"Did you know you woke during the night?"

"I did not!"

Further conversation only caused confusion, and Frisch held back on pushing further as Madeleine raised an eyebrow to remind him that they had been there once before.

~

Frisch has astronaut's dreams.

Saturn sonorously hums a ring cycle. Frisch is held within a metal box amidst the infinite splendour of space. Relatively, there is little difference in the box's dimensions when compared to existence on an Earth contained within the realm of gravity, yet the displacement of the body away from its source imbues him with terror. Frisch is simultaneously agoraphobic and claustrophobic, his nerve ends providing a cycle of expansion and contraction. He can barely bear to exist, yet the alternative is denied. There are no instruments within the smooth walls of the box upon which he might extract his demise.

Neither up nor down in circumstances where *up or down* has no meaning, Frisch drifts in both body and mind, his gaze fixed not on the porthole where the gas giant might itself contain seven hundred and sixty Earths, but to Madeleine who lies almost within reach, his fingertips extended towards hers as though they are stretched on a rack, and within that confinement despite flotation they are as fixed as butterflies on corkboard.

Frisch senses that in this scenario Esme is yet to exist, although there is a distinct sensation that she will enter at any moment, that one side of the box will slide effortlessly upwards and her diminutive form will appear – but not encroach – standing in prescience of her life to come, featureless yet identifiable. She will communicate through that undeveloped mouth some truism which he will recall she has spoken of pre-dream, its actuality all the more horrifying for being banal and having been real. This amalgamation of past / present / future shakes Frisch from the core of his imagination and back to his bed, where Madeleine stirs and fits her hand in his as though waiting for him to wake.

This cooperation of intent coruscates around the edges of a second nightmare with the sound of metal on metal, and when Frisch awakes this time Madeleine's back is turned, and the knowing grin he half-perceived is no longer visible.

~

Esme's tiny fists beat at his chest.

They have experimented with a night-light, torn between practicality and sense. Something garish, with alternating colours shadowing a parade of unicorns and fairies across the ceiling, they consider less conducive to sleep than a simple muted glow. The only concession to gimmick is that it operates under motion detection, leading Frisch to sleep with his eyes fixed on the bottom of Esme's closed bedroom door, as though waiting for a signal in preparation.

The light has made no obvious difference. Esme's contortions are no less abrupt under the soft-spilled spotlight, and in her terror she screams at the source as if it has been directed onto her face under interrogation. When Frisch picks her up she wriggles in his arms, as though his intention is abduction. He recalls Madeleine voicing fears in Esme's earlier existence of waking to find her gone, spirited away either as changeling or experiment, which Frisch had dismissed as fanciful hallucinations from an awakened maternal mind, but as Esme writhes within his grip he wonders at the unnatural expressions on her face, at the disruption of her body, at the sounds coming from her throat. She pummels him as though he is a punch bag. Madeleine appears in the doorway, strands of hair backlit by their own bedroom light, like fluorescent cilia in water.

"You know it doesn't help picking her up."

"What I am supposed to do? I'm exhausted."

Madeleine shakes her head. "She'll come out of it herself."

"It's two in the morning and she's screaming! The neighbours'll think we're trying to strangle her."

"And they'll see us with her later without a scratch."

"You try and sleep through it."

"What do you think I'm doing, standing here?"

Esme's lungs perforated their speech. Frisch returned her to bed, upon which she bucked as though it were a crippled conveyor belt. He placed his hands over his ears. "We can't carry on with this. Let's talk to the doctor again."

Madeleine knelt by Esme's bed, a half-inch from stroking the side of her face, knowing that it would more likely exacerbate than soothe.

They remained in those positions as if in some semblance of tableaux until Esme shushed and slept and they eased themselves out of the moulds they had become in the heat of the night air and returned to their own room and the luxury of peace.

"Remember what he said, that night terrors come from deep sleep, not from nightmare or dream. It's a pattern which cannot sustain itself and ultimately will break."

Frisch turned his back on his wife, not from complaint but from comfort. "I'm more likely to break first," he said, sleep returning to pull on his eyelids, as though drawing the blinds on a particularly busy day.

Madeleine slipped an arm around his waist, her fingers finding his.

"Remember when we thought it was sleep

apnoea? That night we spent waiting for her to stop breathing, possibly hundreds of times? At least we know her little brain is getting enough oxygen, that there are no harmful effects."

But Frisch had by then himself returned to sleep, Madeleine's voice soughing her words into a miasmic blur as though a sonic transformation of a brushstroke across the centre of a painted rainbow, the fibres of the brush collecting an aspect of each colour to render them less unique.

In this instance, Frisch's sleep was dreamless, a subconscious attempt to create Esme's state of mind when she encountered her terrors, however for him there was no journey to the dark night of the soul where all sense of consolation is removed and only anguish results.

Shifting out of bed, Frisch peeked into Esme's room and noted her slumbering form, before descending the stairwell and making his way to the downstairs toilet. Seating himself in the reassuring darkness, streetlight patterning the frosted window in mimicry of kaleidoscopic variations, he rubbed exhaustion from the corners of his eyes and decided that, whatever

Madeleine felt, they should return to the comfort of their doctor's presence and contact him again for diagnosis. Only then would he be satisfied that the contortions of her soft-bodied form might be considered natural and not a result of some exterior fear manifested through sleep. The thought that she might be suffering – subconscious or not – caused him to lie beside her when returning upstairs, her breath shadowing his own as he breathed her in.

~

Frisch dreams of small skin abrasions, surface-scudded damage barely felt until fingers which cut jalapenos skim his arms, the chilli-residue locating each pit with the accuracy of a heat-seeking missile. Despite himself he rubs his hands repeatedly over his limbs, welcoming each sensation of pain in the same instant as being repelled by it. On this occasion he realises he is dreaming, and within that dream wonders if he is making the same movements whilst awake. His consciousness seeks to locate Madeleine in this equation, and the sudden realisation that she might be watching imbues him with a dread he cannot understand. Instead of her presence having a calming effect, his sleep-addled mind finds her a threat, considers that the burning sensation on his skin results not from the chillies but lit matches with which Madeleine purposely smoulders his body hair; each follicle retracting like a surprised conger eel into a pock-marked seascape, her intent unknown and therefore terrifying.

Frisch wakes in sweat on the sofa, one arm trapped under his body: moving it releases blood into his stream and provides a tingling sensation in the limb recovering from numbness. The suggestion that he is not alone carries a fear which is reflected in the recognition of his corporality. As feeling returns to his arm he understands each of the biological processes involved which contribute to this happening. Suddenly desiring to confirm his arm's existence he bangs it repeatedly against the wall above the sofa, until a noise which develops into Madeleine's feet rushing downstairs coalesces into sense and she enters the living room.

"What the hell are you doing? I've just got her off to sleep."

Frisch shrugs off his confusion and regards her afresh.

"I had a nightmare. You were burning my skin."

Madeleine's expression tells Frisch everything he needs to know.

"The doctor will be here in a minute. I still don't see why we have to go through all this again."

Frisch rises, re-establishes a form of identity. "Because it's been five months," he says, stepping closer to Madeleine and leaning in for a hug. "Because her sleep patterns are affecting ours, and these constant interruptions have led to our own circadian sleep disorders. What do you dream, when your nervous system is inactive, your eyes are closed, your postural muscles relaxed, and your consciousness practically suspended? For me, I've reached a stage where the differences between sleep and wakefulness can barely be distinguished."

Madeleine eases away, not without affection. "I wouldn't mention that to Dr Knowles if I were you, he'll have you committed."

Frisch smiles, drops his arms to his sides as though they have been released from a straightjacket. Feeling has returned equally to both limbs. If he thinks about this – *really* thinks about it – he knows he will locate the dichotomy somehow, just as expectation of repetition sustains society, so this is mapped through his bodily functions, and his brain gradually assimilates everything as normal.

They busy themselves in readiness for the presence of Dr Knowles, who Frisch has made sufficiently aware of their distress to persuade him to visit at such an hour. Their house cultivates order, and after an hour where they have almost tipped into a suggestion of relaxation they sit companionably on the sofa and link arms, clock-watching as though at a bus shelter with work a forthcoming destination.

"Recently," Frisch speaks, unable to halt himself, "I dreamt of a young child in a baby seat on the back of her mother's bicycle, her head bobbing from side to side in slumber. I wondered if she were dead. If the mother were attempting to perpetuate her existence through repetition. What do you think to that?"

Madeleine shrugged. "I don't think anything of it. Last night I dreamt of a giant burrito, it's cylindrical shape forming a tunnel which I ate my way through: black beans, red onion, baked Spanish rice, chipotle peppers, shredded lettuce topped with a grilled peach salsa. You were on the other side of the burrito, but you wouldn't meet me halfway."

"You know I don't like burritos," Frisch says, applying logic to nonsense.

They both start at the knock on the door.

~

Dr Knowles removes his hat and places it on the arm of the sofa. He sports a short moustache which Frisch cannot recall from their previous consultation. He is a thick-set man, muscular, not gone to fat. Frisch speculates that Madeleine has estimated his age, filed it away in the back of her mind for purposes unknown.

"Shall we go over what we know?" Dr Knowles is authoritative, yet friendly. "Night terrors tend to happen during periods of arousal from delta sleep, also known as slow-wave sleep. I mentioned before that delta sleep occurs most often during the first half of a sleep cycle, which indicates that people with more delta sleep activity are more prone to night terrors. Esme no doubt falls into this category, and it's perfectly normal for children between the ages of three to twelve to have these experiences. From our previous discussion I think we can rule out confusional arousal. I imagine these disturbances are very upsetting, but Esme will not recall them. My observing her tonight is more to reassure yourselves than to further diagnose her."

Frisch buried irritation, edged by abrasive sleep. "I'm just wondering how long this might last."

Dr Knowles coughed. "Usually night terrors cease upon the subject entering adolescence, although of course..." his voice trailed away, as if dissipating in cloud "...circumstances are different here."

Frisch noticed Madeleine nod. He couldn't disagree with her. Outside the window night pressed its dark face against the glass, an aberrant trickster.

Frisch was about to raise questions over his own dreams, when Esme began her screaming.

Dr Knowles raised his eyes to the ceiling.

"It's the first door on the right," Frisch said. "Are you sure you don't want us to come up?"

"It's best for me to examine her independently, as much as she will allow." Dr Knowles headed for the stairs. "If I need you, I'll call out."

Frisch placed his hand on Madeleine's forearm, sensing her hesitation. "Just humour me this once," he said.

Madeleine returned to the sofa. "What could go wrong?" Her laugh was forced, verging on manic.

Frisch had always understood his wife to be the stoic one, but in an instant he realised Madeleine had been holding it all back: her fears, her maternal instinct, her lack of sleep, her frustration at Frisch dominating their conversations about Esme. He realised that not only had Madeleine been reigning in her worries, she had also been shouldering his own. Tiredness ran the width of her face like an incoming tide, and Frisch appreciated the sacrifices she had made to her sanity for the sake of keeping up appearances.

He sat beside her, sloping an arm around her shoulders. "I'm sure you'll be proved right. I've been over-reacting. It's the lack of a good night's sleep. We've been coping alone far too long."

Madeleine listlessly took his hand. Overhead the floorboards creaked as Esme roiled within her bed, her body pushing the limits of its frame. Her voice loud, incessant, with the tone of an Inuit throat singer, words – if there were such – lost in the vehemence of their expression. The sounds gradually elongated until they were expressed as one long scream which stopped as suddenly as it had begun. The silence exploded with the violence of a nuclear blast: the boom more like a shotgun than a thunderclap, creating a hurricane-eye pause before being followed by a sustained roar.

This second session ended much swifter than the first, with Esme's intonation calming as though the volume was decreased through a music system. Frisch squeezed Madeleine's hand, and they remained silent in anticipation of the sound of Dr Knowles' footsteps as they took each successive step back downstairs.

When the doctor appeared in the living room doorway Frisch was shocked to see his forehead beaded in sweat. Dr Knowles swept a hand through his hair, resetting the style as though in a film played in reverse. He leant against the jamb for a moment, gathering his thoughts. A dark patch on his shirt was evident in the underarm area. Then the doctor stroked his moustache with one finger as though calming an alien entity and said, "I gave her a sedative."

Frisch nodded, waited. There was more to it than this.

Dr Knowles continued into the room, placing his bag on the coffee table. He glanced towards the darkened window, as though taking a cue to continue his conversation. "I stand by my previous diagnosis. It is definitely a night terror, her behaviour occurs on waking abruptly from deep, non-dream sleep. The question is, what causes her to wake?"

"And the answer?" Madeleine untwined herself from Frisch, who noticed a subsequent cooling in his body temperature.

Dr Knowles rested his chin in the palm of his hand.

"I took the liberty of checking her pulse."

"Her pulse?" Frisch stood. "Why on earth would you check her pulse?"

Dr Knowles almost imperceptibly shook his head, as if attempting to understand his own action. "Professional instinct? I don't know. But it doesn't matter. What does matter, is that she had one."

"*She had a pulse?*"

Madeleine's incredulity reflected Frisch's own. They looked to each other and back at Dr Knowles, synchronised in their astonishment.

The doctor's shrug couldn't shift all that he

carried. "It's insane, I know. But during her night terror she held a regular heartbeat. After I gave her the sedative and she calmed then it ceased, it returned to normal."

Madeleine's voice increased to a pitch that strove to emulate Esme's heights during her terrors. "Are you seriously telling us that during these periods she's alive?"

The doctor nodded. "Of course," he began, "this holds implications for everyone. If she is somehow tapping into her past, and it is *this* connection which is causing the disturbances, then..." His voice fell away at the end of the sentence, as though the words to express his thoughts had yet to be devised. Frisch completed the sentence for him, understanding what a valuable commodity Esme might be.

"Of course," Dr Knowles finally continued, "I will have to report this."

Frisch nodded. They had remained standing, although the weight of the discovery had turned their legs supple, the consideration of movement was a threat to break the moment. Frisch could sense reality peeling away from his consciousness like wood shavings. Gradually he turned his head towards the window and the voluminous dark.

"No need to do so just yet," he heard himself saying. "It's late. Perhaps we should sleep on it."

~

There is a field of bright yellow flowers, Esme cannot recall their name, daisies or buttermilk or something quite similar. She skips a fresh trail, her single plait describing an arc as her legs meander sideways, enjoying the freedom to be had in a world just beginning to open up knowledge, to gape into existence at her feet.

Under sedation, brain cells forge connections to experiences shovelled in unconscious memory. Her rhythmic death syndrome jolts her to animation and Esme opens her eyes, finds herself quiet. She pads across the carpet and opens the curtain, just as dawn is breaking. Silently she returns to bed, considers waking her parents.

My Tormentors

She remembered it this way:

Gauzy fog iridescent on her glasses, head turning circles at neon signs coalescing into being with the ferocity of a burn. A bus genuflecting as it discharges into the busy street. Exhaustion clouding the air in a diesel burst. Her fingers clenched into fists through excessive baggage. Then the slow bleed of discovery: the search for shelter, safety, food. The desperation of needing to be alone in the busiest of cities.

When she awakes – yet again – she finds they are standing at the foot of the bed. At this hour they are silhouettes, the thick cloth curtain shielding them from the prominence of the sun. They resemble an artist's frottage, and in memory there is a recollection of their manifestation along similar lines. She raises her head, squints in the shadows. The display on her phone indicates six twenty-two. In a voice not altogether dissimilar from the rabbit which was Frank in *Donnie Darko*, their simultaneous tones urge her to

wake up

She will make protestations, but these are knowingly of no use. Whilst they watch – their gaze never anything but querulous – she reaches for clothes closest to hand. Her underwear stretches with a stiffness common to budget washing powder, her skin itching in retaliation as her t-shirt then jumper assemble themselves over her head. Barefoot, she exits the bedroom with the assistants in tow. The apartment exists on one level, there is nowhere to hide. In the kitchen she prepares sustenance, but any hope that this might diffuse their attention is a temporary fantasy. As they eat she touches the denim fabric of her jeans, slung over the back of the sofa. The fog crept into the material the previous evening, and she cannot quite tell whether they are damp or cold. The same might be said for her skin.

Her assistants had woken her thrice in the

night. The theatre of her eyes has much more happening behind the scenes than their open lenses are willing to admit. A slow ache crenulates her brow. She is fuzzy-sick. Waking segues into disorientation into acceptance. Pulling on those jeans is akin to inserting her legs into drainpipes, the comparison not beyond conscious irony. Whilst her assistants consume, she enters the bathroom, runs a tap. If there are any recording devices in the boxed space then perhaps the running water will deflect.

The window latch is rusted. As she grips, flakes of white paint, hard as plastic, thin as hope, sycamore-fall into the sink. They are two floors high. She absorbs the promise of escape in a drowning man's breath. Imagines herself easing, impossibility-aware, through the rectangular opening. But there is no respite. No sooner does she acknowledge this than the door opens and the assistants are there, waiting.

Can't you see I'm on the toilet?

The words fall like excrement, the lie palpable. She doesn't have to sigh: her every waking word interrogated. Whilst the assistants perform their ablutions, she sneaks a look through bedroom curtains. She has a hankering for a career. Somewhere in the distance – elevated or not – the castle dominates. In the rare occurrence of her assistants being compliant, she will attempt to conquer it. Possibly, even, in spite of them.

~

The pavement is cold hard under the despairing leather of her shoes. Through easy observation it is clear that everyone has one, two or sometimes even three assistants. Whilst there is occasionally a physical distance, it is evident they are tethered. She wishes she might pick up her feet, but the slow grind of existence is a dominant thumb. Her gait echoes in mimicry. At her lowest, the assistants are an antumbra, darkly leaching her personality as though she had ever given it away for free. Morning light gradually picks off the mist as though busting ghosts, sucking dampness dry in the fluid-sperm-wriggle manner of vacuuming ectoplasm. The suggestion of warmth creates a connection between herself and those similar to her, and whilst she is new to this environment – loneliness hunkered over her frame like a sodden overcoat – she steels determination to make a difference.

Excuse me can you
I wonder if I might just
Do you mind, if you have a moment

Yet – just as her pleas are voiced – her assistants – either singly or in tandem – speak over her words, are sonic erasers. The effect is twinned with the ministrations of the assistants of those she wishes to communicate with, until all that remains is some discordant cacophony where reason is buried.

Shaking her head, she finds herself moving forwards, that slim connection of compatibility threading behind her in a genealogical impression akin to geological traces of fossils embedded in sedimentary rock. Out of the span of others, her assistants fall silent, the exchanged glances between them suggestive of *job done*.

So she meanders, the castle present yet inexplicably distant. Stopping at various storefront windows her contemplation is perpetually stymied by the doggedness of the twosome. *Will they never shut up!* she thinks, totally unable to unravel the sense behind their ramblings, their confused logic, their at-odds-with-everything demeanour. At lunchtime – upon their insistence – she finds herself herded into a brightly coloured establishment where the food tastes so much worse than the packaging which contains it; the assistants quaffing and slaking and snorting their drinks with the abandonment of those who are without responsibility, their vigour renewed ten-fold compared to her worn-down expression which she catches in a fingerprint-smeared mirror alongside a bouquet of balloons – perspective lending them her oval visage as though she were contained within a display of Jeff Koons-like Pop Art.

Outside the establishment an attempt at individuality is once again subverted by the assistants, who abuse her suggestion of locating the castle with unsubtle proposals intimating they don't have her best interests at heart. Once again, foot-sore and brain-heavy, she forces optimism into her voice. There is a tacit agreement that their existence is dependent upon one another's, a moral obligation which she cannot override. The assistants – as far as she is aware – are intended to provide her with Buddhist-like revelations of ascendancy. Against all the odds, she clings to her faith in this, her neural pathways glossing over the evident truths of bullying, hounding, their obsessions with unnecessarily meaningless tasks and insistence on sleep-depriving-torture which might undermine the plausibility. If their aim is in fact the erasure of her identity, then might this actually lead to the nirvana of her expectation? Was it not enough to relinquish her worldly goods, but also those intangible qualities from which her character was woven?

Winking, cajoling, mirthful: she cannot tell whether the assistants agree.

~

She performs an experiment. Obtains a pack of playing cards and deals six out in turn, a simple game, which even a child would understand. The assistants rise to the challenge, immediately seeking ways in which to undermine the task. The cards are bedecked with the occupations of those who reside in the city – although those pertaining to herself and the assistants are curiously absent. She queries their intelligence, coerces decisions; and in doing so both assistants confabulate, fabricate imaginary experiences as compensation for an apparent loss of memory. No matter how often she repeats basic instructions, the assistants bicker with regards to meaning, until all meaning is – in fact – contorted, abused, lost.

If only when they slept she might do so too. Yet it is here that a semblance of reality is restored, a necessary resurrection, which the surrealism of sleep could not safely afford.

Sometimes, she watches her assistants meet others of their ilk. They maintain a curious dance of expression, never outwardly sharing experiences, never consciously holding back. These conferences offer no resolution, no concrete advance. Instead of utilising this time to fantasise escape, she snatches brief interludes with others, never voicing the unfathomable pain, the abject despair; instead dreamily focussing on the quirks, the eccentricities which distinguish her assistants from theirs. As if clues might be found in these slight comparisons as to why they adhere to her so. And this process seems part of a passive acceptance, a social necessity obviating her listlessness, normalising her experiences. As if there could ever be anything other.

One afternoon, the sun blanketing those green city spaces in honesty, casting shadows from structures like malformed insects, her assistants taunting her with apparent disdain over their own visions of the castle, she sits on a bench, peppered with hardened spots which don't pick free as easily as flaky-paint, and achieves communion with a pluck of kindred souls in discussion over the likelihood of the existence of that which – by any other name – carries the suggestion of sweet:

A circle of sand, a cocktail, a shark-infested sea

A book. Beginning to end. A book

A lover, uninterrupted, insatiable

None of these marry her vision of ramparts, turrets, corbels, chemises, machicolations, parapets.

How can they begin to revolt when each have disparate goals?

She understands that strength is with the assistants. Their common bond is that of anarchy – and when anarchy has become the prevailing doctrine then there is little chance of coherence amongst those who have been individually displaced. Those affected are walking into a cone, their points of reference diminishing the further they proceed, their posture increasingly cramped, negating any possibility of turning back. The most they can hope for is a fondness of memory, nostalgia for a past barely loosened from the present yet already spiralling in mental pareidolia, stimulating sense where none actually exists.

Her desolation becomes so acute she actually breaks respite and calls the assistants towards her. Grudgingly, they acquiesce, sullen yet flushed. Immediately they resume their roles and she finds herself explaining – justifying – their behaviour, to her previously potential cohorts who are just as incapable as she of upsetting the accepted order of existence.

~

Some days I remember when I used to be my own person.

There is an irony in that she feels she is an amalgam of her assistants, when – in truth – they are composites of her.

Each day they chip away the statue of her despair.

She remembers it this way:

An oscillation of osculation. A nightclub meandering, easy access to her heart. Arms above her head, hips mobile. A presence at her waist. Nods from the door. This is how it begins. There is surety in certainty.

How hard is it to understand that by laying a block to build a castle you have to take it from somewhere other?

Her assistants coax her from the apartment, limbs soft. Her hair, unpegged, gathers in wind. The smell on the breeze is hers. They lead her through streets. Heat like kettledrums. Buildings – all angles and corners – peer around her. Shooting back, as though dissembled, the castle is spied in oddments of brick, grassy passages, those singular spikes designed to prevent the landing of birds, imposing gates, latticed metalwork.

Her face compounded by lack-sleep. Words tumbling incoherently in a sunken trapeze-act of comprehension. Desire a barely perceptible motion.

Throughout one hot summer night, when the air became as slick as rancid butter, when sleep was snatched in fragments like the contents of a communal crisp packet, her assistants took turns interrupting her unconscious state: her nervous system forced active, eyes opened, postural muscles tense, consciousness heightened, she broke:

fuck off! leave me alone! please. please

let me sleep

(crying)

please. just let me sleep

She throws herself to the window, palms flat. Against a gibbous moon the castle manifests into being, a metaphor of salvation. She grabs each of the assistants, pushes their struggling, uncomprehending, expressions towards the glass.

Do you see it?

Can you take me there?

I could just reach out and

That night she sleeps under the windowsill, the duvet from the bed a cocoon for an unlikely butterfly, her assistants nestled close, as though the castle's apparent proximity makes for a tangible release. Regardless of the heat, there is warmth in the symbiotic relationship. She understands the prevailing view that she might have no purpose without them, that they certainly would have no purpose without her. If she dreams, it is from the comfort of strangers.

Yet – come morning – the heat-haze mirageing such a solid brick edifice, her assistants resume their squabbling, their inconsistencies, their torment. Like a particularly virulent form of tinnitus their remonstrations invade her head, the residual warmth threatening to circle her with a spiral, constrictive not open-ended. There is an echo from the night before, a twitch of anxiety. She waits whilst her assistants find the clothes with which they would prefer to be dressed. Her own garments have seen better days, have seen better.

They intrude on her every waking moment with their ugly, pointless proclivities. She loses the momentum of yesterday. Even the simplest question becomes a battle. Her legs give. Ineffectively her assistants tug her from the parquet. Their mouths streaming.

When she raises her head, she sees the calendar taped to the wall. In just a few months, the heat will be sucked from the city, the daylight hours will sharpen, diminish. The chances of locating the castle in darkness, without sunlight sparking from the edifice, will decrease. The time spent with the assistants, enclosed in whatever fresh atrocity they will invent for her, will stretch malodorously. She feels her skin edging beneath her clothing, a virulent craving. With certainty she rises, silently, enters the bathroom and turns taps.

With promises of something other she

persuades them from their clothing. She will sluice this cancer. She has had the right – and she has known this for some time – to pursue her desire. And it is a right. A certainty.

Warm water captures her assistants, bubbles bobsleigh their bodies. If they laugh, it is directed towards her. If they smile, perhaps that too. There is almost a speckle of bliss as she kneels beside them. Almost a family. Yet she requires more than a temporary respite, as oil-skeins make concave pods for slickness, and she pushes the first one down into the depths.

She is up to both elbows in it. They slosh against her offence.

When the residue of soap retracts on the surface, like a shrinking of ice, as though the unveiling of masks following a particularly fretful masquerade, she finds the bodies aren't quite still. Fluid motion displaces, discolouration in the water. Buoyed by physics without independent movement.

The tightness within her eases as she lifts her assistants from the space. Their anonymity no longer shrouds. She knows them as well as you do.

And in that she finds relief.

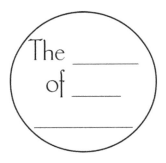

The _____
of _____
_____

1. _____

Emma spent the remainder of the summer reading through the literature and making her final decision. It had been seasonably hot. The endless holidays of her youth telescoped into the present, compounding memory. She found herself inventive in the ways which occupied Oliver: they spent time in the nearest park, enjoyed a week with her family in the Cotswolds, participated in several activities arranged at the local library, and followed the trail of fibreglass creatures which had been placed around the city and which would later be auctioned for charity.

Oliver was a studious five year-old, curious and demanding. The volunteers at the pre-school had suggested he was bright for his age, and Emma couldn't help but agree as he sounded out letters phonetically and then strung and fleshed each combination into individual words and sentences. Emma couldn't remember if she was as precocious at his age, but she doubted it. In those days, even the word *precocious* was viewed as an insult, as though being clever beyond your years was something deliberate and to be ashamed of.

Gary had encouraged Oliver through books. At first the baby basics: black and white animals voicing *moo* or *baa*. Then the more complex scenarios, with gaily colourful insects trailing a path to be followed by an inquisitive finger, towards a flower whose petals might be peeled back to reveal a bug or the smiling face of a friendly spider. The longer picture books came next. Oliver preferred the comical stories, those which carried their message via a laugh rather than those which were overly moralistic in tone. These were the best books to read and read again. Like most children, Oliver was into repetition in a big way. At his age, it wasn't simply a process of reinforcement but also an indication of how, through necessity, his outlook was narrowed. Emma considered this carefully, how we begin closed and then open up to the world only to gradually stake our boundaries and close down again.

She would have conversations with Gary where they agreed that their formative years were those spent in adolescence, where world views were harnessed to the parental structure over which they had little control, but which used that framework to bounce further into speculation and create hard and fast opinions which – however absurd or relevant – would always be difficult to shake. She had been drawn to Gary because it appeared there were similarities in their ways of thinking, and as they got to know each other better – through touch, heartbeat, the satisfaction of sexual impulse – these similarities were not only made visible but became entwined. The rest, as they say, was history.

Engagement. Marriage. Pregnancy.

Oliver was a planned child. Not for him an inglorious bastard. He had also been a rare child, emerging from Emma's vagina fully inside the amniotic sac, the thin and filmy membrane explained as an *en caul birth* by the midwife as she gently peeled the casing away.

Emma smiled as she recalled Gary's expression, the unfamiliarity of the experience running a vein of horror through his gaze which transmitted itself to her, through an association with fear, until she held Oliver to her breast and he began an easy suckle. They found it prophetic, too. When the midwife asked if they had an interest in keeping the caul the answer was unequivocal. Whilst they had never shown it to Oliver, they kept it in a sealed container; first underneath his cot and then latterly his bed. Gary had researched superstitions about the caul on the internet, and had discovered that in some countries placing a caul under a dying person's bed was believed to make their passing easier. Other old wives tales were less appealing, and whilst those born with a caul were considered safe from drowning, neither Emma nor Gary felt inclined to put that to the test.

Early autumn sunlight crazed through the bay window and spotlit Oliver's school uniform, hung over the back of a dining chair. Grey trousers, white shirt, red blazer. When Emma was a child formal wear had only been a matter for High School, but she understood the logic, the urge for homogeneity, safety in solidarity.

She wished Gary could see Oliver on his first day, stood to attention, posed for a photograph against the kitchen wall, their little soldier ready for battle.

Despite him not being home, Emma knew it wouldn't be long before Gary saw the photograph. She imagined the pride swelling in his heart as he shared the image with those around him.

It was still early. Emma switched on the television and then left the room to look for her hairbrush. Voices from the set grew fainter the further she moved around the house, as though someone were slowly muting sound. Once she found the brush she ran it through her hair until she couldn't disguise her dissatisfaction, then she parted it down the middle and plaited it either side. By the time she returned to the living room Oliver had woken and crept downstairs, his face illuminated through the reflected glow of a cartoon. When Emma was young, *Tom and Jerry* were wiry adversaries, now they were baby-fat chubby and playacting violence. There was a time when parents and children would watch cartoons together. She could imagine that time no longer. She entered the kitchen and poured out a bowl of Cookie Crisp cereal. It was Oliver's favourite, and only fitting that he should have it for breakfast this morning. He would have chosen it, regardless of her decision.

She placed the bowl on the low table in front of him and he spooned mountains into his mouth as milk dribbled down his chin.

"Careful sweetheart."

She could turn off the television, but mornings were easier with it on. The programmes regimented the routine. Oliver knew once this set of cartoons was finished that it would be time for school. They had practiced the procedure during the holidays: get up, have breakfast, get dressed and out of the door by seven-thirty. Timings were important. She didn't want him to be late. If the cartoons distracted, then it was both a welcome and unwelcome consequence.

Duality was everywhere. It was in love and then it was in something else.

She brushed Oliver's hair as he ate. It didn't take much to keep him in order. Unlike her hair, which tangled at any opportunity.

Emma remembered passing the brush to Gary one morning, as she sat on the edge of the bed and he was in the process of waking. He regarded the wooden handle and stiff bristles as though it were a foreign object, before smiling and pushing back the covers, kneeling behind her in his boxers and then gently brushing her hair as if it might disintegrate in his touch. She showed him how to use the brush roughly, to tease out knots with effort, until her body jerked backwards and he held her in his arms, their laughter as exultant as the birdsong beyond the window.

Slipping out of her dressing gown, changing her underwear, stepping into and then zipping up a freshly-ironed dress, Emma considered why it was often necessary to be harsh when handling life. Those knots wouldn't undo themselves.

There was a phrase, she considered as she applied her make-up, heard when she was younger: *spare the rod and spoil the child*. One of her school friends who attended church had quoted Proverbs: *He who spares the rod hates his son, but he who loves him is careful to discipline him.* But it was Becky who was scared of her father, whilst Emma adored hers. She wondered how this background might form the basis of speculation. Returning to Oliver in the living room at the close of *Tom and Jerry* she understood the difference between violence and cartoon violence. Not everyone could distinguish those subtleties, or were willing to attempt so.

Oliver had drained his bowl. She deftly wiped his milk moustache and stood him on the sofa as she pulled down his pyjama bottoms and then unbuttoned and slipped the top over his head. Freshening him with a couple of wet wipes she changed his underwear and socks and had him dressed in his uniform within the space of the adverts before Oliver settled down for a final cartoon.

Folding his pyjamas and then popping them into the washing machine, Emma entered the kitchen and carefully checked the contents of his lunchbox.

She imagined Gary standing behind her, his head nestled against her neck, as she went through the motions for the umpteenth time.

"Such an important day."

"It'll be fine."

"Life will never be the same again."

"Hopefully, for the better."

Checking the time, she clipped the lid shut

and packed the box into Oliver's backpack. Running the cold tap Emma filled his water bottle and then stood it within the bag. On a whim she picked an apple out of the fruit bowl and added it to the contents, smiling as she did so.

It was a nice touch.

She didn't even need to turn off the television. Oliver had already done so, as though he were attuned to her clockwork. She bent to kiss him on the forehead and was about to slip the backpack over his shoulders before deciding it was better to carry it herself. The nerves were building, expected. Taking a quick look at her surroundings, she opened the front door and they left the house. She noticed Oliver had picked up a biscuit on his way out, palming it ineffectively in his hand as though it were some big secret. She wouldn't begrudge him that.

The morning was Indian summer hot. Vapour was exorcised from the pavement and drifted skywards, as though ascending souls. Spiders' webs held dew droplets in elaborate filigree. Oliver felt for her hand with his and she clasped it, a key entering a lock. He began chattering, and Emma returned responses with well-timed accuracy, her mind elsewhere, considering all possibilities. If Oliver noticed her inattentive attention he didn't voice it. Emma could sense his excitement, burred by bravado and trepidation. They were alike, just in that moment, in the short walk to school. Each of them wearing a face not quite true, subtle nuances of anxiety popping under a surface sheen.

Each step compounded inevitability.

It had been Emma who had suggested this city, Gary nodding thoughtfully as she scrolled through properties online. It was of sufficient distance to curb any friendships that they had, and out of the catchment area of the nursery school which Oliver had previously attended. In making this decision Emma understood that she had set the ball rolling, nudged herself into pole position when it came to decision making. Gary hadn't stepped back, but she had stepped forward. It was important to him, she realised, that through motherhood she had taken control. It put them on an even keel, paved the way for complex discussions in the aftermath.

As they walked, Emma watched other parents and their children congregate towards the school in a V, as though hauled towards their destination in a fisherman's net. The metaphor was apt, she realised, and at that moment looked down to Oliver's hand clutched in hers, a hand which slowly broke away as they were joined by other children, the fingers disengaging as if to say *this is just not cool any more*. As his hand left hers completely so did any vestige of culpability.

They were inside the compound now. The primary school had three entrances for six separate classrooms. Emma had already flagged an anxiety condition to the staff so that they were aware she wouldn't be accompanying Oliver into the building. *He's an independent lad*, she had said, realising as she did so that she would never have used the word *lad* when describing her son. *He'll find his way in with the others, no problem.*

Dropping to her knees just inside the gate she turned Oliver around and fixed the backpack over his shoulders. In the distance, another parent – a man – caught her eye and instantly she felt flustered, until she realised that in the crouch she had shown rather too much leg. She returned the stare, made it one to remember, then kissed Oliver on his forehead and turned him back like a clockwork soldier.

"Off you go."

He looked over his shoulder, seemed to contemplate giving her a hug, but with a quick nod of her head he appeared to understand the futility and then merged into the crowd.

Emma walked back towards the main gate. She glanced at her watch. It would all be over in a matter of seconds. Too late to stop it even if she wanted to.

At the gate, the headteacher, Ms Fry, had made a belated appearance, meeting and greeting a few stragglers whilst the bulk of the children and their parents were now congregated by the classrooms. There was almost a palpable sensation of excitement in the air, voices creating a tsunami crescendo of sound. Ms Fry noticed Emma and attempted a smile, but when she opened her mouth to say something her voice was subsumed by the severity of the explosion as it ripped through Oliver's lunchbox, peeling exposed skin away from nearby faces in filmy membranes, and returning parts of Emma's son to her.

Her ears rang, just like the temporary tinnitus she had been subjected to after a gig she had attended with Gary. *Nirvana* had been the name of the band. It was their second or third date. The second, come to think of it. But after a few hours the noise had abated and it had no further effect on her life. She knew the ramifications this time would be different.

With pandemonium around her Emma spoke softly under her breath.

we sacrifice our children for a better future

The lipstick on Ms Fry's expression formed a perfect *O*.

~

2. ___

Max had struggled to get to sleep but when Julia broke into song, gradually quietening her voice in delivery, his eyelids drooped and he was away before she finished the first verse. In the moment, she continued until her song was complete, singing to keep awake rather than to doze on the bed alongside him.

It was a chill night. Whilst Max had been tucked in, she had been dressed in a short blouse and denim skirt which had proved insufficient as the sun vacated the room. Standing, shivering, she rubbed each shoulder with the opposing hand, and then grabbed a cardigan from her bedroom before returning downstairs where Ben was tapping away on his laptop.

"I think I've found some," he said. "Don't know why I didn't think of it before. eBay."

Julia raised her eyebrows. Sliding into the narrow space beside him on the sofa, she glanced over at the screen. Five seeds, not dissimilar in colouration and size to kidney beans, were depicted in the palm of a hand.

"These are definitely the ones?"

Ben nodded. "*Physostigma venenosum*." He smiled. "I've been working on the pronunciation."

She squeezed her left hand through the gap between his right arm and chest, and squeezed again as an act of love. "Calabar beans, yes?"

Ben nodded again. In the steady glow of the standard lamp illuminating the room Julia's legs were attractive against the blue of the denim. He hadn't always felt that way. There had been pockets of discontent in the relationship which had mirrored global politics, but he had a feeling their fortunes were turning. If he wanted to be facetious, he might equate the beans to the fairytale story of *Jack and the Beanstalk*, but whilst he had circled the thought he had never decided to include it in conversation.

Julia wouldn't have thought him serious. But he was.

"What's the delivery date on those?"

Ben scrolled down the screen. "They're coming from Germany. Should be here within the week. Are we doing this?"

It wasn't even a question. The beans were £7.90 plus £2.48 delivery. Neither of them would raise an argument to that.

Once they had turned the downstairs lights off and checked the doors were locked they used the bathroom alternately, and Ben entered the bed whilst Julia checked on Max in the next room.

"All quiet?"

Julia nodded.

She slipped off the cardigan and then reached under her blouse at the back to unclip her bra, glad to be rid of the thing. Ben had already sensed the moment and she could see the movement of his hand under the sheet. She climbed onto the bed beside him and knelt so that her palms were pressed deep into the pillow on the other side of his head, bridging. He knew how much she liked her nipples sucked through the material of the blouse, and when he touched her there with his lips, gently at first then with increasing urgency, the night closed around them to the detriment of all others until they emerged spent and smiling and huddled in close.

Occasional car lights made a shadowplay on the opposite wall. Julia remembered an evening in Bali in the town of Ubud. They had ditched the tour party and wandered pleasantly, aimlessly, eating nasi goreng from a street stall and pineapple from skewers. Whilst it was late there seemed no cessation of activity. They purchased sarongs and immediately wore them, congratulating themselves on going native. Unlike changes of temperature back home, the humidity created a sensation of constancy over the evening, to the extent that they felt it was permanent.

Towards midnight they followed the locals towards a patch of coarse land, in the centre of which a screen had been erected. Julia gripped Ben's wrist when she realised it was a puppet show. They had intended to see one with their tour party, but this appeared much more authentic. Afterwards they would laugh when recounting the evening as story, not having realised it would be a ritualised midnight-to-dawn show, but in the moment – as part of the mysticism to which they surely thought they were being aligned – they sat fascinated as the puppeteer entertained, the audience sitting on both sides of the screen.

It had been that same morning, after the conclusion of the show, when they finally returned to their bed covered by the filmy membrane of the mosquito net, that they had fucked and conceived Max.

Ben was sleeping. When Julia closed her eyes she could almost see figures projected onto her lids, until eventually the cocoon of their house contained no one that was conscious.

Max was a bright, inquisitive boy. When the package eased its way through their brush-sealed letterbox he carefully put down his crayons and wandered out to the hallway to see what had landed.

The padded bag appealed with its texture. Max pressed down on it with his fingertips, enjoyed the soft-flexibility of the material. Inside, the beans were well protected enough for damage, but when Julia came downstairs after tidying his bed she had to fight the urge to snatch the package out of his hands and shoo him back into the living room. Clutching it to his chest, Max beamed at her, a smile which would warm any heart, and Julia smiled back, holding that position until Max passed over the package without the need for coercion.

"You're so cute," she said.

"I *know*. You keep *telling* me."

She watched as he returned to his drawing, a deeply-scored spray of red resembling arterial blood, then entered the kitchen and tore back the flap before tipping the contents into her palm.

Within their see-through plastic covering the beans appeared innocuous. She turned them over a couple of times without removing them, and then on tip-toe placed them on top of the Brabrantia container they used for teabags, well out of reach of prying hands and eyes.

For a moment she stood, motionless, as if she were thinking and the effort had decapacitated her body's nervous system, and then – almost as though she were a clockwork toy returned to motion – she closed the cupboard door and walked across to the calendar.

The beans had arrived in good time. Max would be four that Saturday.

Julia spent the remainder of the morning in the living room with Max, reading a magazine whilst he continued his drawing, making the right noises now and again. Max wasn't a skittish child, prone to tantrums or explosions of energy, but introspective and absorbed. Once he had made a decision as to how he would spend his time, he remained steadfast in his work. Julia considered he was similar to Ben in that regard. Whilst Ben ensured he saw every project through, she would need prompting. This was no doubt the reason she had remained out of work since the pregnancy, she considered, as she selected a *Golden Barrel* from the tub of *Roses* she kept near the magazine rack. Even so, she had been applying for jobs, wary of the downturn in the financial sector.

After lunch she wrapped Max up and took him to the park. Despite the increasingly chilly nights the day burnt autumnal hot, and she found herself unwrapping him again before they had walked a hundred yards. On the swings Max urged her to push him *higher higher*, and he laughed when she sat on the other side of the seesaw and couldn't get up again, his legs swinging back and forth in the air. Julia exchanged a handful of nods and the occasional pleasantry with other parents in the vicinity, but in effect Max isolated her within a bubble of her own making, and she was grateful to him for that.

If there was fear, it came in the shape of the slide, an antiquated design with a caged winding staircase which suddenly opened at the top, revealing a precarious step before a body might safely sit on the shining polished surface of the descent. Fate was a heartbeat either way each time Max bridged the gap. Julia considered these moments quite seriously, wondering how soft the sand would be given a fall. It interested her that Max had no such perception of the fear, and that therefore for him the possibility of falling didn't exist.

She wondered if it were the impression of danger which parents imposed on their children which allowed the actuality of such dangers to exist.

Later, they sat on a bench and removed their shoes, tipping sand onto the grass.

There was a cat in the park, Julia noticed. It

was odd to see it in such a location, although she couldn't quite place why. She realised from its movements that it was toying with something: it shot out its paws, fumbled them together as though puzzling a Rubik's Cube, and then drew them back into its body again, before rising and slinking low in a semi-circle and repeating the pattern. Max hadn't noticed and Julia wondered if he would. From time to time, she glimpsed a small brown smudge against the background of grass. No one else appeared to have noticed the cat, they were occupied with the playthings in a similar fashion. When Max returned his shoes to his feet he became attuned to where she was looking.

"What's that?"

She chose her words carefully. "A cat and a mouse."

"Oh."

Max rose from the floor and wandered over. Julia stood. Indecisive.

The mouse seemed unperturbed by the game. Whenever the cat withdrew it raised its paws to its face in the process of washing. There was no blood, no apparent injury. Then the cat was upon it again.

"Mum."

There was more to the word than the descriptive. Julia found herself intercepting the cat in its movements with the mouse, placing her foot in the space in-between, although such a stance appeared to offer no difference. The mouse would dart off, then attempt to hide in the grass. The cat would walk around Julia's foot and find it again. Eventually they both disappeared under a hedge and Julia ushered Max away.

"They've stopped playing now," she said. But what she meant was that it was no longer a game.

Ben showered before dinner. Julia heard him switch off the water as she plated up the food. Max used an old cushion to reach the dinner table, and they were halfway through their meal before Ben made an appearance.

"Mmmm...lasagne," he said, ruffling Max's hair and kissing Julia on the cheek. It was such a parody of suburbia that Julia had to laugh.

Later Ben put Max to bed, and when he returned downstairs Julia had retrieved the beans from their safety place and was turning them over in her hands, their hard surfaces sliding against the plastic membrane which contained them.

"These arrived."

"So I see."

Ben reached for them as Julia held them high, slightly behind her head where she reclined on the sofa, so Ben had to reach into her to grab them and she surprised him with a kiss.

"Naughty."

"You wish."

Ben split the plastic and shook out the beans, turning them with his fingers.

"Innocuous enough."

Julia nodded. "You'd think so."

"How are we going to know if they'll work?"

She shrugged. "When we know, it'll already be too late."

Ben turned his head towards the stairwell, captured by thought. "I guess so."

The remaining days stuttered by, some hours relegated to seconds, some seconds promoted to hours. There was urgency within the household. Julia and Ben took it in turns to initiate their lovemaking, as though through a repeating pattern they might channel some luck. If they took control of the night, then Max held charge over the day: his play appearing more focussed to Julia, more assertive, as though he had an indication that a moment was coming, that something was expected of him.

When Saturday came Max was unaware it was his birthday. Julia and Ben had agreed there was little point in cluttering the day, degrading it with an excitement unbecoming. Max woke them as usual, created a car from their bed, buried himself under their covers and hid. He laughed when Ben suspended him in the air, flexing then jerking his arms to send him skyward. Julia rose and prepared breakfast: eggs and beans and some bacon that was close to better days.

They left the house mid-afternoon. Autumnal sunrays kaleidoscoped leaves, their shades darkening and lightening as they crisscrossed each other in the breeze. It was a lengthy walk through the woods to the hillock. Max ran ahead, kicking leaf-fall with red Wellington boots, climbing tree stumps, tripping and tumbling. Julia held Ben's hand and he hers. They were comparatively silent, each condensed in thoughts shared with the other without the need for vocalisation.

The hillock's historic significance was limited to their personal experience: they had fucked there once. A daring, carefree afternoon, where the anticipation of being discovered had heightened their activity. When they had discussed places to perform the ritual the hillock was in the forefront of their minds, as if their act that day had the sole purpose of signposting it for the future. And once again, the possibility of discovery would add frisson to their actions.

They had prepared sandwiches – just in case – but had underestimated Max's curiosity. He chewed each bean slowly. Whilst they sought from his expression an understanding of the taste, Max was as methodical in his actions as their intentions were deliberate. Julia considered it was almost as though he knew what they were doing, although this was impossible. She had come prepared to disguise the beans, to force them if necessary, however Max continued to be adorable until the end.

The hillock extended above low-lying foliage, hidden within a circle of trees. As the sun bowed to the horizon, Ben leant forwards and wiped Max's forehead, checked his reduced pupil size, then leapt backwards as Max voided his bowels and vomited simultaneously. Max became weak in that moment, as though it were sickness that had been expelled from him instead of the ichor Julia and Ben had anticipated, then his face assumed an angelic countenance and their momentary worries fled.

As the alkaloid physostigmine acted like nerve gas, confusing communication between Max's nerves and his muscles, Julia opened the picnic basket and removed the saw.

She looked to Ben, then. With the sun to his rear he appeared as a silhouette, features indiscernible, until the subtle shift of the Earth's curvature revealed him once again. Julia wondered how she had appeared to him. Whether her pupils had dilated in the presence of the light.

They held each other's hands, then, as practised, in the bedroom, in the kitchen, in the living room – they spoke in unison.

we sacrifice our children for a better future

The sun had wholly set by the time the sacrifice was complete.

~

3. ____ & _____

It was after one particularly busy Christmas, when their children received as many presents as could reasonably be afforded, that Carly and Patrick decided to scale back.

It was New Year's Eve. The children were staying with grandparents. Carly and Patrick were snuggled on the sofa, a tube of Pringles either side with a half-emptied bottle of red between them. They were staring into space, each succumbing to individual thought, wine glasses clutched between their fingers, enjoying a rare evening of quiet, when Patrick voiced what they had both been thinking: "It's a proper shithole in here."

Carly laughed. Her eyes had also been drawn to their children's Christmas presents, which still hadn't been transferred to their rooms, and which spilled over the living room carpet in disorderly piles.

"I'm serious. Someone needs to do some cleaning up."

Carly dug him in the ribs. "*Someone?*"

"Not *someone*, obviously. *You.*"

She glanced at the clock. It was only eight thirty-five, several hours til midnight, when they might acknowledge the New Year and slide themselves into bed. Without children the evening had started early, and now they were struggling to know what to do with themselves.

She sat up. "You're not serious, right?"

Patrick sighed. "Not about you. That bit was a joke. A poor one, admittedly. The real joke is the mess in here."

Carly nodded. "I was thinking it myself."

"We need to downsize. There's too much stuff we don't need. Not the new toys, obviously. But a lot of what we have should go."

Carly reached for her Pringles and pushed her hand in up to the wrist. "Spring cleaning?"

"All I'm saying is that we'd be a lot happier with much more space."

Patrick reached for his own tube. Carly never liked the sour cream and chives flavour, whilst for him it was the only kind worth having. He popped a half dozen crisps into his mouth and crunched through them like a demolition machine scrunching through six abandoned floors. "It's like these crisps," he said, mouth full, "we don't need them, but they're here so we're eating them."

"It's New Year's Eve. A treat."

"Hardly a treat. I'm bloated and feeling the effects. We've had these almost every night this week."

Carly could feel the waistband of her PJ's digging into her stomach. The trouble was they were so moreish.

"It's simple really," Patrick continued. "If they weren't in the house, we wouldn't eat them."

Silence accompanied them for a while, save the processes of digestion, as each weighed up the options of crisps versus no crisps. They hadn't even put the television on. The intention had been to enjoy a quiet evening to themselves, but in place of conversation they had been drawn to food and drink. It hadn't always been that way. Carly realised Patrick was right: they needed to de-clutter.

"Okay," she said, "it's New Year's Day tomorrow. Symbolic. Let's make a list."

Patrick rose to find paper and pen. "The sooner we stop buying crap the better. Let's live within our means."

They spent the remainder of the evening in furious debate, determining what they could and couldn't part with, whilst the seconds that crept into the new decade remained uncounted.

Liam and Charlotte had been less than enthused. Charlotte in particular had always been something of a hoarder, retaining packaging and broken toys which were anathema to disposal. Patrick sweetened the pill by suggesting the proceeds from a car boot sale could go into their pockets, ostensibly to buy new toys. But whilst Charlotte wanted new things, she wanted her old things too.

Liam was more pragmatic. His approach went along the lines of *if I give up A B C can I have X Y Z?* He was the older child, almost nine whilst his sister was six. Yet Patrick had noted what constituted *A B C* was far smaller than the gleam of the *X Y Z* in his eyes.

Both children were beyond the age whereby a swift tidy-up in their absence might result in their 'old toys' having 'gone into the loft'. A white lie, which both Carly and Patrick had used on occasion to stuff twentieth century detritus into the bin. The problem was the quantity. Charlotte in particular favoured blind boxes with innumerable plastic figurines in; collecting a whole set involved potential re-mortgage, and each finish line was suddenly extended by an additional range of *specials*. What made matters worse was the keeping of the packaging, which invariably was three times bigger than the contents to dull parents into believing there was actually some worth to be had.

In Liam's case, his room contained enough Lego to build a second room inside it. Each set to be created by preordained designs, lest imagination might lead to a less than satisfactory construction.

Add to this innumerable computer games, swiftly obsolete technology, toys whose advertisement – similar to movie trailers – belied the usefulness of the product, and it soon became apparent that the slow accumulation of unnecessary paraphernalia was a serious problem which needed immediate rectification.

"They go on," said Patrick, "about all the plastic floating in the sea, but that's got nothing on what we're dealing with in this house."

So days passed in determined attrition, with Carly and Patrick frequently remembering and enforcing that they were the parents and homeowners when it came to disposal; their efforts stymied by internal battles coupled by the influence of external forces.

"The trouble is," Patrick said, one evening

after the children were asleep and the television was without solace, "that we can afford this."

Carly understood. She had fought Charlotte's corner for her recent birthday when it became apparent that their *new toys for old* placebo was expected to be fulfilled.

"We're mortgage free and without debt. We have disposable income. Society wants us to dispose of it. It's a spiral."

Patrick nodded. He stood and began to pace.

"I've been thinking of reducing my hours at work."

A tremor of apprehension skewed Carly's spine. "You've spoken about this before."

"In the context of spending more time together. But this is...different." He paused. Looked her in the eyes. "If we don't have it, we can't spend it."

Carly understood. She had spent some of her free time researching downsizing and knew that they were at the base of a cone. The further they journeyed to reach the point, the narrower and more constrictive their lifestyles would become. She was eager for it.

"To be honest," she said, "I considered stopping work altogether."

Patrick watched as she rose and embraced him in a tight hug. Whilst her voice was faint, there was determination to be had.

"Let's derail this train completely."

Their lovemaking that night was particularly vigorous.

Liam noticed the changes first: a lack of chocolate in the refrigerator, his Dad home when he returned from school, fewer arguments about insignificant things. There were changes in diet. Shops' Own brands with their distinctive indistinctive packaging crowded the cupboards, although Liam could taste no discernible differences. He made a scene at first, particularly when it came to crisps: *I'm not eating those!* But normality was a blanket that covered a sleeping child, and what was unusual soon became natural. If he found himself hungry more frequently, he was advised to drink a glass of water. After a few days the ache diminished and reduced food intake began again.

Charlotte became grumpier the hungrier she became. Carly found it much more difficult to deny her needs, occasionally sneaking her a biscuit here and there which she would have denied Liam. She wondered about these allegiances, whether it was innate to protect a daughter over a son, but these were mild aberrations and Charlotte soon settled into a routine of eating less, and then eating less healthily. They switched from farm shop pork and apple burgers to twenty coasters for a pound in less than a week. It was all mechanically retrieved, but Carly soon decided not to read the fine print on the packaging. They lived within their means and then they further reduced their means. It wasn't anti-capitalist, just anti.

Being out of work benefited their free time, although Carly struggled to find use in it. Their social lives had taken a dive when Patrick was born, and hit the bottom of the pool head first when Charlotte arrived. New sets of friends with children had been foisted upon them, and it was almost a relief to cry off with poverty, yet the moratorium on shopping also confined them to the house, and it wasn't long before they had run out of boxsets to watch, which shortly led them to cancel their various pay-per-view subscriptions.

One morning, slouching in tracksuit bottoms and contemplating whether to bath, Carly began to cry.

"What is it?"

Patrick had taken the children to school and was spooning a knock-off version of Kellogg's cornflakes into his mouth.

"I just feel so...so useless."

He rose and put an arm around her. "I know. I love you."

"I love you too, but it doesn't help matters. Have we done the right thing?"

Truth be told Patrick wasn't sure, but he said: "It's a social experiment, that's all. We need to cut back what we don't need, and if we were in work it would be much harder. We had this discussion."

"I know. But is this how everyone feels?"

"Others don't have the vision that we have. You remember what we discussed, that evening when we decided to give up our jobs? You remember what we decided this change of circumstances would justify?"

Carly nodded. How could she forget it.

"So we'll hit rock bottom and then we'll raise ourselves back up. When it's over we'll sell the house, move elsewhere and start afresh."

Carly dried her eyes with her sleeve. They each had these moments of doubt, of unbridled fear. Only last week she had comforted Patrick and mouthed similar words. It hadn't gone beyond her notice that it had been the morning they had advised Liam he wouldn't go on the school trip. Children added guilt where none should be placed. It was societal demands which stressed families, coherence to the norm. It would be all too easy to give in, regain employment, and levitate with the kids. But that would achieve nothing other than to return them to exactly where they had been. They needed to lose ballast before they would rise.

So she let Patrick comfort her and run her a hot bath. Afterwards he caressed the bones beneath her skin and she traced his ridges under her fingertips. They were paler, she knew, sallow in complexion, but the rut continued to find them and they rode the changes well.

They made the decision to home school the children after seven months, coinciding it with the start of the summer holidays. Malnutrition had yet to set in but they knew the children would have been subject to the scrutiny of outside forces which could now be denied them. They were an intelligent couple, advised Services to Home Educators, who were not there to dissuade them, simply to tick the box that the children had opportunities at home outside of mainstream schooling. Carly and Patrick had smiled. There was less chance of discovery, and their project could begin in earnest.

When Carly suggested they confine the children to their rooms, Patrick didn't disagree. Their finances were meagre now, stretched out like elastic so that they weren't elastic any further. They sold belongings for food: the sofa, games consoles, widescreen TV, dining table. Carly made a fair bit from designer shoes and dresses which increased their heart rates a little, like the blip of a cardiology machine, and Patrick sold his tools – remarking as he did so that the process of sloughing their respective purchases also flatlined their stereotypes. They sold the newer toys last, once Liam and Charlotte were too weak to object. You would think they had sold their internal organs by the way skin clung to their bones, as though shrink-wrapped onto wire frames. Barely membranous.

"I nailed their windows shut," Patrick said one morning, Carly's eye barely open; watching him through the gauze of unwashed hair. "Liam had been trying to get out."

Carly nodded. Her lips were cracked. There was a hunger in her belly which she understood as a knot. It was strange how clichés revealed their truth the more frequently you prodded them.

Patrick stroked her forehead. His fingers held no moisture. The last time Carly had seen her children their legs were the same width from ankle to thigh, covered in scratches and bed sores. Patrick then took over. It wasn't that she hadn't the resolve, but the knowledge they had gone beyond medical help cast a pall she couldn't shake. She felt guilty, knew that it wasn't easy for Patrick, that he too was suffering the same.

She remembered *Hansel and Gretel*, how the children had been led into the forest because the family had insufficient food to survive, yet somehow they had defeated the metaphor of the witch and returned to embrace their father's love. She wondered if the gingerbread house represented delirium dreams, whether the happy ending was a construct of the subconscious to facilitate their journey into death. She understood that unlike them, in the fairy tale the parents hadn't deliberately run down their finances to justify killing their children through the need for survival, but the parallel was sufficient to give her strength.

"How long?"

Patrick shrugged. His skin shifting on his frame like an oversized overcoat. "A few days."

She struggled to move her body to one side, to lean on her elbow. "We'll do it now then. With pillows."

Patrick nodded and helped her rise. They took the stairs hand in hand, their shadows ascending Nosferatu-like and slender.

Carly released Charlotte first. Her body reduced to nothing.

Liam took longer. But then it was also done.

we sacrifice our children for a better future

Without the expense of their offspring they scraped enough to continue. Gradually, Patrick and Carly restored their health.

4. _____

It was on his third visit to Dr Gilbert to discuss Loren's increasingly difficult behaviour that Adam realised he was falling in love.

Dr Amanda Gilbert wore round-framed

glasses over a moon-shaped face. Her hair was cut short, and her flowered shirts were long enough to be dresses. On each occasion she appeared flushed to see him, her lips barely brushed with rouge. Adam was under no delusions that she viewed both him and Loren as a problem waiting to be solved, but there was acceptance in her friendly manner which made him realise how health professionals must tread a thin line between caring as an occupation and caring as an expression of interest.

Loren was fourteen. Her mother was somewhere else with someone else. She excelled at school and was destined for Oxbridge: a term Adam had always considered strange as it was both no place and some place. She had a small circle of what appeared to be close friends and enjoyed a good book, particularly Facebook. This was the joke he usually told to introduce his daughter and to break the ice with potential partners; it didn't often crack a smile. Dr Amanda Gilbert had raised an eyebrow in comic appreciation.

Adam had taken Loren to the GP surgery due to a change in her eating habits.

"I don't understand. She used to enjoy all

kinds of food, but now she insists on sandwiches for lunch and dinner. She skips breakfast entirely."

Dr Amanda Gilbert smiled at Loren as though she had told a joke, and then said: "I knew a girl once who lived on crisps for two years. It never did her any permanent harm."

Adam had almost shook with puzzlement, then he saw a glimmer of acceptance cross Loren's expression and he realised that in a couple of sentences Dr Amanda Gilbert had opened Loren's worldview to accept that what she was doing wasn't particularly unusual or worrying. This was the polar opposite of Adam's own approach, which had been to condemn her for not eating *normally*.

"Is there any particular reason you can find as to why your eating habits have changed?" Dr Amanda Gilbert asked.

Loren shook her head.

"Would you rather talk about it with your father outside?"

Loren shrugged. Adam said he wouldn't mind. Loren stared at the floor.

"What should I do?" he asked.

"Nothing for now. She's a healthy girl. This is

perfectly normal behaviour for children of her age. Don't push her into anything and she'll likely find her way out of it. If you continue to be concerned about the health issues or the behaviour escalates then please make another appointment."

So Adam did.

Dr Amanda Gilbert admitted him with a *Hello. Is Loren not with you?*

Adam shook his head. "I made the appointment in her name, but she wouldn't come."

"Perhaps she doesn't think it necessary?"

"That's what she says."

"And why are you here? For reassurance?"

Adam imagined reclining his head against Dr Amanda Gilbert's chest and her fingers gently stroking his hair as she reassured him.

"I still don't know what to make of it."

"Have you noticed her being sick, deliberately? Or eating more than usual, regardless of the type of food?"

Adam shook his head.

Under patient confidentiality Dr Amanda Gilbert declined to mention to Mr Adam Chandler that Loren had made a solo appointment to discuss contraception. She had completed a pregnancy test in the surgery and it had proved negative. Dr Amanda Gilbert could link a minor eating disorder to the fear of motherhood and had little doubt that life would soon stabilise for her patient. Loren had been open to suggestion, and Dr Amanda Gilbert had laid a seed to be cultivated at a later date. Under patient confidentiality there was no necessity to identify that seed to her father. However she did find herself contemplating that Mr Adam Chandler was an interestingly handsome man with a rogue's face, who presumably had had little luck with finding a partner since his wife's departure because of the presence of a precocious child.

On his third visit – after Loren had stayed out all night without 'remembering' to text him – after Adam had been frantic with worry and realised he didn't have any contact details for any of her friends – Dr Amanda Gilbert found herself allowing him to rest his head upon her chest as his body fluttered with exhausted sobs and her fingers gently raked through his hair.

The diagnosis was of a single father realising that his daughter was on the brink of sexual awakening, and of a single-minded daughter understanding that her father could never be her mother.

Dr Amanda Gilbert realised she was skating on thin ice. Loren was her patient, but Mr Adam Chandler was registered to Dr Gary Calcutt and she had never attended to him in a professional capacity. She could argue – if it were needed – that technically she had not crossed a doctor-patient boundary, that Mr Adam Chandler was not vulnerable and potentially exploitable. But she hoped that she would not have to offer such an explanation, because his vulnerability and exploitability were exactly why she had chosen him.

They kept their relationship secret. Most often they would meet after work for an hour, arriving at their destination in separate vehicles, usually in the countryside considering the weather was so clement, and Amanda would guide Adam's body against her own under a sky so brilliantly blue that it hurt her eyes to look at it.

Loren had made two appointments with Amanda since the relationship had begun. The first regarding depression as a result of online bullying, and the second to raise concerns about a persistent tummy ache. Amanda had used these occasions to initiate a special bond between the two of them, engaging in a role of confidante which went above and beyond professional interest and veered towards friendship. It was clear that Loren saw in Amanda aspects of a mother she had barely known, and when Amanda suggesting bloodletting as a potential cure for both stomach ache and depression, the girl was naïve enough to accept this without question.

Amanda made the first small cut on the roof of Loren's mouth with a scalpel so sharp Loren didn't register any pain and only realised the procedure had been concluded when she tasted copper in her mouth.

Loren was encouraged to bend over a clear plastic bowl as the 'bad blood' dripped from the open wound. Amanda invented an experience of being bullied at school which she had overcome to succeed as a GP, in order to create empathy and to further ingratiate herself in Loren's good books.

That evening when Adam exposed her breasts behind the bale which hid them from the traffic, Amanda recalled the Facebook joke and smiled at a connection that only she could make.

Afterwards, Amanda stuffed the spent condom into the bale, forcing it deep inside, the tightly packed weave of hay pressing hard against her fingertips.

The irregular menstruation caused by successive occasions of bloodletting gave Loren frequent worries about the effectiveness of contraception. This led to a cycle of visits where Amanda increased the frequency and duration of the bloodletting, alternating cuts from the roof of the mouth to Loren's back, chest and stomach. Each cut was sufficiently diminutive to avoid discovery, which Amanda equated to the development of her relationship with Adam.

By endowing her interactions between each of them with an element of secrecy, Amanda knew neither would tell on the other for fear of breaking a special spell. Furthermore, Adam would defend her should her intervention with Loren come to light. It would be more complicated should Loren discover the liaison with her father, but considering Amanda's relationship with Loren was time-critical she hoped that wouldn't be the case.

It was after several months, following the

course of various appointments in which Amanda had persuaded Loren to provide a snippet of hair together with a photograph, that she had collected Loren after school and driven her to the cemetery.

Autumn was settling in. The sun was sufficiently low in the sky to refract dangerously against her windscreen, and Amanda narrowly missed a cyclist who appeared to materialise at close quarters. Loren was clutching a positive test for pregnancy which Amanda had switched for that of her own when Loren had turned to get dressed, and she further displayed symptoms of being distraught due to a resurgence of the bullying she had once experienced online.

"Some people draw bad elements to themselves," Amanda said, as they parked the car and walked to the oldest section of the cemetery. "In times gone by, they might be considered possessed or to be a witch. We don't have to believe in that for it to be true or otherwise. We simply need to believe we can do something about it in order to empower ourselves."

Loren nodded meekly. She considered herself an intelligent child, not prone to madness nor superstition, but she was also open-minded enough to understand there were forces which couldn't regularly be explained. In her youth, knowledge was perceived as purely the tip of the iceberg, with most adults denying that the bottom was in existence.

When they reached the area Amanda had scouted as being safe from prying eyes, she removed the plastic wallet within which she had sealed some of Loren's blood, hair, and the photograph, and passed it to Loren to make the oath. The blood discoloured the image, attaching itself to the hair in the simulacrum of a membrane.

For Loren, the cursing ritual guaranteed her freedom, happiness and prosperity. For Amanda, the oath guaranteed her Loren.

we sacrifice our children for a better future

Loren was fully coerced into subservience by the time Amanda had begun to show, her disappearance suspected by police to be linked to human trafficking and sexual exploitation.

When Loren's body was discovered the following Autumn, harvested in a hay bale, Mr Adam Chandler's grief was compounded by the simultaneous news that his estranged girlfriend had that morning birthed a daughter.

5. The _____ of ____ _____

There is extensive documentation to suggest that forest atmosphere has a wholesome effect on our emotional state. It helps to relax and calm, improves stamina and sleep, eases confrontation and allows for tolerance. Research suggests that if someone should spend even a few brief moments in the forest, it would be enough to improve the functions of their central nervous system, lift their mood, and restore their vitality. Qualified practitioners of forest therapy carefully facilitate programmes which are uniquely tailored to the needs of each individual and have the fundamental aim of building each participant's self-esteem, confidence, independence and creativity. In each instance the forest does not need to refer to an actual place – even an imaginary forest plays an important role in purification – but to the philosophy of an ideal:

Have children act out the lifecycle of a tree. They can curl up as a seed, kneel to sprout, stick arms out like branches, wiggle fingers for leaves, stand up to grow tall, spread feet to show roots, and fall over to die.

Call our number for further information.

The
Harvest

Tate buried her in sand.

Whilst his wife was alive they rarely visited the beach. Helen hadn't enjoyed the sensation of loose granular material seeping between her toes, as though seeking to engulf her, regardless of footwear. At times, during her final cancer death throes, Tate considered the disease not to be dissimilar from sand. The way, like water, it permeated.

Once their daughter, Hannah, was born, beach visits had ceased altogether. Helen was convinced crumbling fistfuls would find their way into Hannah's mouth, that it would seek the otherwise soft crevices around the folds of her skin, that somehow it might pour out alongside her breastmilk. Even during the hottest days, with swift breezes running off the tips of the sea to deceive those without lotion, Helen preferred their garden sanctuary. She would rock Hannah's Moses basket with the tips of her toes as they dangled from the sunlounger, whilst Tate would shield the glare from the white pages of a book, or alternatively buzz around the lawn pushing the blades of the mower.

Since her death, times at the beach were bittersweet. Almost a *fuck you* to Helen and the disease which had taken her. Tate was in mixed-minds as to whether the cancer had been a curse or a blessing. Their marriage wasn't as it used to be. The moment of Helen's diagnosis opened up vistas which he had assumed had forever been denied.

So, with Hannah giggling, he felt no guilt in spading heaps of sand over her feet, as the sonic Bank Holiday Monday roared around them in the guise of day-trippers of all hues and class, the hubbub a threat to the sky, their bodies splayed over the stretch of yellow which on cooler days appeared to extend beyond sight.

Hannah wriggled her toes, and the smooth surface crenulated then buckled as though a highway distorted through earthquake. Another laugh: her browny-blonde hair, knotted in places, curved fetchingly around her face; her perfect teeth evenly spaced in an innocent smile; her freckles almost visibly erupting like the rust spots which were no doubt forming on his vehicle scoured by salty air.

Again! Again!

Tate laughed, too. Catching the eye of a woman sunbathing under an angled umbrella, having exchanged a series of muted almost non-existent signals suggestive of ellipses over the previous five minutes, he dug into the sand with the spade and placed his feet deep into the resultant hole, before Hannah pulled the tool from his grasp and filled it in. She patted the sand down with her feet – he could barely detect the pressure – then willed him to reveal each toe, shrieking this time in tandem with the gulls that coursed overhead with a persistent vision of ice-cream and chips.

The sun bore down. The sunbathing woman's husband returned and any connection between them – imagined or otherwise – was lost. Tate looked at sea. The percentage of those bathers within the water was infinitesimal when compared to the vastness of churning liquid. He took Hannah's hand and they made their way towards the froth, squeaking as the occasional stone scuppered their gait, before gradually immersing the tips of their bodies into the coolness of the suppurating waves, body temperature gradually lowering to that of the water, until eventually they warmed.

He pulled Hannah's hat from the pocket of his shorts, depositing it on her tousled hair. She shrugged it off twice before understanding there was no argument. Tate's own head was bare – hair sparse, receding – and he knew that in the evening the skin would tighten like the proverbial drum, which he would painfully remember until he dried himself after a shower, and then recollect all over again.

Hannah skimmed stones. Tate remembered Helen being averse to this activity, arguing that an object which had taken several millions of years to make it to the beach shouldn't be summarily returned. Tate had accepted this as part of their relationship, that any progress would be slow – almost intolerable – whereas returning to their starting point might happen in a moment. Under Helen's influence, he still deferred participating with Hannah, who skimmed stones badly, uncomprehending of the wider picture.

Her hand was tiny in his. Just right. Five years old, articulate, absorbing, Hannah was on the cusp of realisation when it came to the influence she exerted over him, and – in a process of parasitical empathy – he welcomed this and the relationship between them had fully blossomed.

If the shadow of Helen's demise tore a black cloud into the day, Hannah appeared oblivious to it. Her natural acceptance to the scheme of things had been purely animalistic, without the heavy-hearted taint that adults bore around the subject of death. As yet unaware of her own mortality, Hannah's understanding of her mother's absence was simply functional. Tate felt comfortable in the manner with which he had shielded her from the worst of it, and indeed Helen herself had thanked him profusely as she sank into the abyss, urging a final promise to – *of course* – take care – *of course* - of their daughter.

Tate glanced at his phone. He no longer wore a watch and felt bereft without one. The time had edged beyond twelve, acknowledged by the ache in his stomach and the increase in day-trippers disgorged from the miniature railway which ran along the spit on hourly journeys, ferrying those too late to find spaces in the absurdly crammed carpark. They needed to return by three. There was a football match Tate wanted to catch, and despite the joy he felt in spending time around Hannah, there were only so many orders he could take. Hannah would welcome the coolness of the sofa, watching videos or playing games on her tablet. It would enable her to wind down, and if they left the beach too late there was always the threat that she might drift asleep on the return journey, a fear which Tate was convinced would add several hours to the bedtime rituals should she claim ten minutes in powernap.

He tugged on her hand and she wrenched her fingers free, scrabbling for pebbles just under the water which jostled on each incoming around her feet.

Just one more.

Tate arced his back, stretched as though assessing the sea. So many layers of water, one atop the other, so much unseen. He returned to their towels, roughly sandpapered his feet until they were dry enough to enter his socks, and then slipped on his shoes. He moved their towels off the main drag, placing them atop a rounded wall which acted as a sea defence, before returning for Hannah and plucking her out of the waves, her body contorting in anger and then placating with the promise of food and the allure of the joyrides. Tate sat her on the low wall whilst he ran the towel as gently as possible over her feet, grains sticking to her skin like impossibly tiny molluscs.

~

The rides were cheap enough to entertain without placing too much of a demand on his wallet. Hannah rode an undulating green serpent along a bright red metal track, waving each time she passed his wave, his other hand holding his phone as he filmed her excitement. Capturing such moments – committing them to permanence – made him feel Helen's absence quite acutely, as though her desertion were more of a presence – as though she existed *more* in those moments where Hannah might also continue in perpetuity. However Tate was accomplished in avoidance techniques and he pushed Helen's memory to the back of his mind, a place where the good and bad of them argued for dominance, where the good usually won out during the dark hours of the night when Hannah was finally asleep and Tate appreciated just how alone he was and how much Helen's non-existence was keenly felt.

However he tried to dissociate, tears usually came.

The ride concluded, Hannah begged for the Tea-Cups and was spun gracefully by a sympathetic fairground worker who was long attuned to the scale of screams which – according to each child – indicated the speed at which the course might be set. Tate flicked his gaze around the other holidaymakers, simultaneously discounting future mates as too boorish, too local, too young. Once the ride concluded, he spent the last of her tokens on The Big Slide, watched Hannah haul the cumbersome woven mat up steps which would have had Helen's fingers over her eyes, until she reached the top and – as though she had done so since birth – capably arranged the mat and then her legs into the correct position, before gripping the straps and jiggling her bottom until momentum – aided by a freshly-waxed surface – took hold and she whizzed downwards, bouncing and rising with each plastic hump, finally spooling sideways at the bottom and looking at Tate eagerly, seizing the nod which meant she could repeat again and again.

They ate chips at an uneven metal table – fashioned, perhaps, out of the armour of King Arthur's knights – before wandering the few shops to kill the remainder of their duration on the parking ticket. Tate surveyed the timeless tat: A4 Elvis posters, Marilyn Monroe coasters, Red Indian figurines and headdresses, miscellaneous items stamped with familiar names of either gender, and t-shirts sloganed (in)appropriately depending on target age. With time becoming a premium, he scooped Hannah up and away from a trinket dispensing machine with the promise of an ice-cream, which they then ate on the walk back to the car, Hannah's melting fast over her fingers until Tate's handkerchief was wringable by the time they were finished.

He had taken Hannah to the loo shortly after they had left the beach, and – checking that she didn't require it again – he strapped her into the carseat, her body succumbing to the curves of the material, her face almost flaccid in exhaustion, his mind accepting that sleep would

– in fact – be inevitable, and his free time that evening would become truncated by a resurgence in energy. Still, it didn't matter. It had been a *good day*, one which he hoped she would remember.

Sitting behind the driving wheel a sudden pressure around his own bladder after fixing the seatbelt made him realise he had yet to urinate. Tate sighed, readied himself to unbuckle Hannah and carry her across to the car park toilets, to navigate the stench inside, and then to return and strap her in once more. Weariness clouded the fringes of his consciousness, and he looked back to see that Hannah, too, had become drained by the intensity of their day.

He glanced at his dashboard clock. It was two-fifteen. Their ticket held five remaining minutes. He had forty-five minutes to make the thirty-minute journey before the start of the game. Closing his eyes, the sun made orange halves of the interior of his eyelids. *Hannah*, he heard himself saying, *are you ok to wait in the car whilst Daddy goes to the loo?*

In the rear-view mirror he watched her nod enthusiastically, welcoming the intimation of trust. He considered what he had said. That tiny conversation would mark the end of her childhood and the beginning of adulthood. From this moment forwards, there would never again be a hesitation in leaving her in the car; like Helen's cancer, the fact of its existence opened new possibilities.

Tate sought a reassurance, then unbuckled his seatbelt and left the vehicle. Smiling somewhat amateurishly, he closed the door and – without hesitation – locked it. The toilets were in view, it wouldn't take more than a minute. Along the boundary of the car park fairy lights twisted in a simulacrum of barbed wire. He moved further and further away from the vehicle, carried by a swirl of fate, until he entered the concrete building and succumbed to a fatal heart attack inside one of the stalls, his urine continuing to discharge even after his death.

~

Hannah watched until her father was out of sight, then she leant to her left with a view of releasing herself from the seatbelt. She wanted to hide in the footwell, to surprise him when he returned. He would pretend he couldn't see her, and there would be a moment of total complicity, before one of them would break and reassert some reality to the situation.

Her fingers pushed hard on the release button and it shortly gave under pressure, the belt retracting quickly and catching her slightly against the soft underskin of her chin. She gave a little squeak, then shifted herself off the seat and squeezed her way from the back to the front, crouching down passenger side where her mother's feet used to tap rhythmically against the rubber mat whilst something poppy and cheerful played on the radio. It was hot down there, stifling in fact, but Hannah held a chuckle inside and curled into a ball, ignoring the thick smell, the handful of wrappers, the excitement of discovery, the toxic oppression.

Whenever she hid this way time appeared longer than it was. She had yet to gain a grip on hours and minutes, but if her body were a sundial it would be twelve o'clock, the position she had assumed created an angle which delivered the best of the sun's rays through the glass windows as though it had remained the height of day.

And as she waited, sleep claimed her.

Her eyelids hung like anvils, her tongue making ineffective forays against the dryness of her lips, her skin shrinking against her frame, sweat pooling on her skin and depleting salt during its exit, nausea keeping her still.

Kaleidoscopic light blossomed sunflower patterns filtered through orange, dark yellows, and deep browns. Hannah chased the colours, splashed them askance, was aware of a freedom of futility in a never-ending summer. Heat buckled her memories, imbued her dreaming. Butterflies gorged with shadows of dust echoed in vast landscapes. A rainbow of sorts cut a swathe into her vision. There was a turgidity to her thoughts as she considered running towards the curve, subconscious-soup thick. She intimated a craving of beauty, a rush to the ethereal. She felt her body relax, uncurl, lend itself to the moment, accept the fluidity of released tension.

Her limbs ghosted over brilliant white daisies centred with yolk-round spots, buttercups coated slick, poppies edging with the brittleness of crepe paper, with tiny breathing hairs. In the distance: mountains, peaks, sky. Tumbling: blue replaced green replaced blue. She accentuated her thoughts, pushed against the reverb, freed to elasticity. Stretching wilded her; swimming in air she called the name of each animal, watched as they attended her, from the fowl to the beast, the fur to the horn. Their tiny fingers bristling with Sellotape and humour, with the blatant respect of everyday.

Her ears accepted the veracity of the tumult. Sounds commingled in waves, as though under water, a distortion of voices. Considering this immersion her body racked a breath, a bubble of snot. She flipped over, coasted backwards, plastic deposits within translucent eggs writhed their possibilities. Twisting and halving, she disgorged their contents: an amalgam of sheen. Figurine maps flitted on sheaves of paper. Unable to make the match, she closed her eyes yet saw them all the same. Rivulets of liquid between her toes. The grit which takes an oyster to pearl.

In one ascent she beautifies the sun, the brilliant white orb which surrenders subtle manna, watches her skin distend as though under a blowtorch, a flame erupting from an unattended chip pan, a coruscation of bruises, a yielding to ferment.

Moments of clarity punk her wisdom. Words drip from picture books. Something akin to chewing gum traps and finalises her position. She turns within the gel. An automatic animal. Fissures disguise synchronicity. Minerals hike in exit. Something thick, right in her mouth: a pale whale trapped between banks of cracked earth. A dark pressure distends her hearing. Voices emerge from the tumult: *Han Han Ah Ah*. There is no grip to them.

Something inside her yearns. A forgotten fight. Music runs a tangent in her mind, the *V* of progress punctuates her vision. Solid colours appear in tandem, random; chunks of viscous. They congeal, absorb themselves into gaps, squash whatever view she has. Imitate the heat until they are one and the same. Scour her throat, spin her, tumble simple hallucinations.

The flail of her mind forces logic onto entanglement. She patterns familiarity: her school, her home, her room, her mother. She impresses these rubbings, these certainties, like clutching water in uncupped palms, or encouraging sand to filter through her fingers.

Then the lucidity vanishes. She witnesses a shade of diaspora, a fermentation of dispersal.

Fragmentation / carpet-deep / funnel-friendly / *can't take this now.*

Her imagination grows a sunspot, a region of reduced surface temperature caused by concentration of magnetic field flux which inhibits convection.

She slips beyond in pure hallucinogenic heat haze.

And then

Also by Andrew Hook:

Novels
Moon Beaver (ENC Press, 2004)
The Immortalists (Telos Publishing, 2014)
Church of Wire (Telos Publishing, 2015)

Collections
The Virtual Menagerie and Other Stories (Elastic Press, 2002)
Beyond Each Blue Horizon (Crowswing Books, 2005)
Residue (Halfcut Publications, 2006)
Nitrospective (Dog Horn Publishing, 2011)
Human Maps (Eibonvale Press, 2016)

Novellas
And God Created Zombies (NewCon Press, 2009)
Ponthe Oldenguine (Atomic Fez, 2010)
The Green (Snowbooks, 2016)

Visit Andrew Hook at his website:
andrew-hook.com

*Now available and forthcoming from
Black Shuck Shadows:*

Shadows 1 – The Spirits of Christmas
by Paul Kane

Shadows 2 – Tales of New Mexico
by Joseph D'Lacey

Shadows 3 – Unquiet Waters
by Thana Niveau

Shadows 4 – The Life Cycle
by Paul Kane

Shadows 5 – The Death of Boys
by Gary Fry

Shadows 6 – Broken on the Inside
by Phil Sloman

Shadows 7 – The Martledge Variations
by Simon Kurt Unsworth

Shadows 8 – Singing Back the Dark
by Simon Bestwick

blackshuckbooks.co.uk/shadows